LIBRARIES NI
WITHDRAWN FROM STOCK

MICKY's
Mag

D0589660

MICKY's
Magic Pencil

Vivian French

Illustrated by
Sarah Jennings

Orion
Children's Books

First published in Great Britain in 2014 by Orion Children's Books
This edition published in Great Britain in 2015 by Hodder and Stoughton

3 5 7 9 10 8 6 4 2

Text © Vivian French 2014
Illustrations © Sarah Jennings 2014
The moral rights of Vivian French and Sarah Jennings to be
identified as author and illustrator of this work has been asserted.
All characters and events in this publication, other than those clearly
in the public domain, are fictitious and any resemblance to
real persons, living or dead, is purely coincidental.

All rights reserved.
No part of this publication may be reproduced, stored in
a retrieval system, or transmitted, in any form or by any means,
without the prior permission in writing of the publisher, nor be
otherwise circulated in any form of binding or cover other than that in
which it is published and without a similar condition including this condition
being imposed on the subsequent purchaser.

A CIP catalogue record for this book
is available from the British Library.

ISBN 978 1 4440 1178 4

Printed and bound in China

The paper and board used in this book are from well-managed forests
and other responsible sources.

Orion Children's Books
An imprint of
Hachette Children's Group
Part of Hodder & Stoughton
Carmelite House
50 Victoria Embankment
London EC4Y 0DZ
An Hachette UK Company

www.hachette.co.uk

For Sunita,
with much love, Viv x

Contents

Chapter One

On Monday morning Micky
rushed into the classroom. "Look
what my gran sent me! It's a
magic pencil!" he shouted.

Class G crowded round.

"It looks like any old pencil to me," said Molly. "I don't believe it's magic."

Micky held up the pencil.
"It **is** magic! Watch!"

He grabbed a piece of paper
and drew a circle on it. The
circle was red and yellow and
blue and green, and it sparkled.

"Wow!" said Pip. "That's brilliant! Can I have a go?"

Micky hesitated. He wanted to go on drawing, but he liked Pip a lot. "OK," he said.

Mrs Grant came into the room. "Good morning, everyone."

"I've got a magic pencil!" Micky told her.

"How lovely," Mrs Grant said.

Class G sat at their tables, and Mrs Grant went to her desk.

"We've got a busy day today," she said. "Maths first."

Micky groaned. He didn't like maths.

Mrs Grant smiled at him. "Never mind. You can use your magic pencil."

"Pip's got it," Micky said. "Can I have it back, please, Pip?"

Pip was using the magic pencil to write in her new homework book. "Look!" she said. "It writes really well!"

"That's because it's magic," Micky told her.

Molly shook her head. "There's no such thing as magic."

"Yes there is," Pip said. "Look at my writing!"

Mrs Grant went to see. "Goodness, Pip! That's very neat! Would you like to hand out the maths worksheets?"

Pip beamed. "Yes please."

Molly frowned. She liked handing out the worksheets.

"See, Molly?" Micky waved his pencil in the air. "I told you it was magic!"

Chapter Two

Class G sat and stared at their worksheets.

"I really don't like maths," Micky said. Even though he had his magic pencil, the sums looked hard.

"I do," said Molly. "I love maths! I'm really good at adding up, aren't I, Mrs Grant?" She made a face at Micky. "I don't need a silly magic pencil!"

Zak began to cry. "I can't do it," he wailed. "The numbers are stupid!"

Micky looked at Zak. A tear was rolling down Zak's cheek.

"Cheer up," Micky said. "You can use my magic pencil."

Zak sniffed. "It won't work."

A moment later he looked up with a huge smile. "I can do it!" he said. "Sixteen apples and five apples adds up to twenty-one!"

Molly stared at him. "But you're no good at maths!"

"I'm good at it now," Zak said. "I can do the next one too. Nine and eleven is twenty! Would you be sick if you ate twenty apples, Mrs Grant?"

Mrs Grant nodded. "I think you might be, Zak." She put two big ticks in Zak's work book. "You're as good as Molly!"

Micky turned to Molly. "See? I told you it was magic!"

Chapter Three

The next lesson was P.E.
Micky and Zak walked to
the hall together, chatting.

"We'll be using the skipping ropes today," Mrs Grant said. "Who likes skipping?"

Lots of hands went up.

Maisie slunk to the back of the line. "I hate skipping," she whispered to Zak and Micky. "I always fall over."

Micky beamed at her. "Here! Put my magic pencil in your pocket!"

"I love skipping," said Molly. "Watch me do doubles!"

"We'll all skip together," Mrs Grant said. "Everyone ready? Let's begin!"

Everyone skipped. Molly did doubles . . .

And then Maisie did doubles as well.

"Look what I can do!" she said in surprise.

"Wow!" said Molly. "You're almost better than me!"

Micky grinned. "That's because Maisie's got my magic pencil in her pocket."

"Give it to me," Molly ordered. "If it's really magic I'll be able to do a million skips!"

But she couldn't. "Huh! I knew it wouldn't work!" She dropped the pencil on the floor.

Mrs Grant said, "Maybe it helps people who think they can't do things, when really they can." She smiled at Maisie.

Maisie nodded. "That's right! Watch!" And she did ten doubles in a row.

At lunchtime everyone wanted to sit next to Micky.

"We're doing the Victorians this afternoon," Billy said. "Can I use your pencil for drawing a coal mine?"

"Can I use it for writing a poem?" asked Ben.

"Can I use it for my newspaper report?" asked Asif.

Micky sighed. He'd been hoping to use his pencil himself.

"Please?" begged Billy and Ben and Asif.

"OK," Micky said. "You can take it in turns." Then he said to Molly, "See? I told you it was magic."

Molly sniffed. "I don't need it anyway," she said.

Chapter Four

At the end of the day Mrs Grant looked at the children's work.

"Wonderful!" she said. "You've all done very well. Micky's pencil worked real magic! Thank you, Micky."

"That's OK," said Micky. He looked round. "Where is it?"

"I haven't got it," said Billy.

"Nor me," said Ben. "I gave it to Zak."

Zak shrugged. "I haven't seen it for ages."

"Maybe Asif's got it?" said Pip.
But Asif didn't have the
magic pencil, and nor did Danny
or Jade or Dylan or Daisy or
George or Sasha or Keira.

"Everybody have a proper look," Mrs Grant told them.

"Check your work trays, and look under all the tables and chairs."

Class G jumped up and rushed round the classroom.

"I've found a stripy pencil!" shouted Jade.

"I've found a pencil with a rubber!" yelled George.

Daisy waved a pencil in the air. "I've found a spotty one!"

Mrs Grant clapped her hands.
"Hush! Everyone sit down."
She sounded cross. There was a sudden silence. "That's better," Mrs Grant said.

Pip put up her hand. "Please, Mrs Grant — I think I might have found Micky's magic pencil . . . but I'm not sure."

Chapter Five

Pip was holding something. It didn't look much like the magic pencil Micky had brought into school.

Or could it be?

It was the right colour.

Micky rubbed his head and stared. It was VERY small.

He made up his mind. "That's not my magic pencil," he said. "It's too tiny!"

Mrs Grant looked as well.
"Actually, I think it might be." she said. She drew a wavy line on a piece of paper, and it was red and yellow and blue and green, and it sparkled.

"But what's happened to it?" Micky asked.

Maisie went pink. "Um . . . I did sharpen it. Just a bit. And that made it a teeny tiny bit smaller. But only a teeny tiny bit."

"I sharpened it too," said Asif.

"And me," said George.

Sasha and Daisy nodded. "We did too."

"I sharpened it as well." Pip held up her pencil sharpener. "I sharpened it twice."

Micky picked up the stub of the pencil. "Oh," he said.

"It's all used up," Sasha said sadly.

"Micky was very kind to lend everyone his magic pencil," Mrs Grant said. "I think we should all say sorry."

"Sorry, Micky!" everyone said together.

Micky dropped the end of his magic pencil in the waste paper basket. "It's OK," he said, but his voice was a little bit wobbly. "I don't really mind."

Zak went over to Micky. "Tell you what, Micky. Tomorrow I'll bring you a new red pencil because you were so kind to me today. It's not a magic pencil, but it's a very nice one."

"I'll bring you a blue one,"
Pip told him.

"And we'll bring a green
one," said the twins.

"Yellow!" shouted George.

And the rest of the class all
promised Micky different colours.

Molly came over to Micky too. She was holding out her favourite blue sparkly pencil.

"You don't have to give me anything," Micky said. "You didn't use my magic pencil."

"Um." Molly went pink. "Actually, I did. I used it to write my party invitations."

She pulled a card out of her drawer. "Here you are. Can you come? Everyone else is."

"Thanks," said Micky. "It looks really nice."

Molly went even pinker. "I'm sorry I didn't believe you, Micky. Actually . . . actually, I think your pencil really is magic."

Micky grinned, and picked up his school bag. "Good. See you all tomorrow for another magic day!" And he went out of the door, whistling cheerfully.

What are you going to read next?

Have more adventures with
Horrid Henry,

or save the day with Anthony Ant!

Become a
superhero with Monstar,

float off to
sea with
Algy,

or have your very own Pirates' Picnic.

Grow carrots with

Lottie and Dottie,

make magic with
The Witch Dog,

and cast a
spell with

The Three
Little Magicians.

Enjoy all the Early Readers.

the orion star

CALLING ALL GROWN-UPS!
Sign up for **the orion star** newsletter to hear about your favourite authors and exclusive competitions, plus details of how children can join our 'Story Stars' review panel.

Sign up at:

www.orionbooks.co.uk/orionstar

Follow us @the_orionstar
Find us facebook.com/TheOrionStar